When Melvin the Camel Meets Donald Trump

By Cody Visnick and Bruce Ackerman

The stories in this book were developed as a collaborative method: One of us begins with a paragraph or two, then Granddad or Cody develop it further, then passes it on until we hammer out something that sounds good? Granddad began using this method since his kids, Sybil and John, were very little, and over time, all his grandkids have joined in – creating characters whose personalities have become part of the family!

While Granddad and Cody made up these particular stories, we owe a lot to other tales created by Cody's stepsister and step-brothers, Sammy, Bella, and Lucas. That's why these three characters play such important roles in this book. Thanks a lot for the inspiration – we love you!

Chapters

Becoming Melvin

Melvinopolis is the only city in the universe inhabited entirely by camels. It is in a lovely spot on the planet Murth, 18 million light years away from Earth.

Charlie was a lonely camel living in the outskirts of the city. He tried playing with other kids but they always beat him up. Whenever they played war he tried to make peace and no one liked that idea.

One day he was sitting down for lunch and he saw a small dot on the horizon. It got BIGGER and BIGGER. It landed 3 meters from where he was eating.

He examined the space ship. It was weird. It was a reddish purple, and it was mostly short except for a hundred meter high control tower sticking up.

He saw four figures casually

climbing down the ladder from the control tower. They opened a huge door and rolled out on the first dune buggy in the history of the planet Murth.

"What is that!?" shouted Charlie.

"Who are you!?" shouted the four creatures.

The creatures were very much human children and they had never discovered intelligent life on any other planet.

"Where did you learn English?" asked the four kids.

"At the Intergalactic Institute for

the Study of the Universe," said Charlie, very proudly.

"What are your names?" asked Charlie.

"Bella, Lucas, Sammy and Cody."

"Who's who?" Charlie asked.

"The tall one with the brown hair is Bella, a teenager. Lucas and Samantha are twins and Cody is about the same age as the twins, twelve."

"Cody's the one with the blond hair, Lucas is the taller boy with the shorter haircut and Sammy's the girl with the long brown hair."

As they were talking, they saw two camels walking along the road, mumbling to one another.

BIG camel said to the other camel, "Here's eight million hay buckets. Take the money and I want you to make it legal for my family to be the only seller of food in the city."

The other camel had a crown on his head. He was the governor of Melvinopolis for the next two years. He nodded his head and said, "It's a deal!"

As the two camels walked back to the big city, the four kids asked,

"What's going on here?"

Charlie translated since BIG and the Governor were talking Cam-Cam, their native language.

"That is completely bad!" shouted the kids.

"That is a perfect example of corruption. What are we going to do about it!?" Cody said angrily.

Charlie shook his head and said, "I don't think that we can do very much. When I tried to make peace among the warring kids, they beat me up. These guys are much more powerful. They'll do something awful to us. We have no chance."

"Actually, we have a security camera on our ship. We recorded that entire conversation," said Bella.

Charlie was still very uncertain: "You don't know how awful these guys are."

"We have to try to clean up Melvinopolis!" declared the kids.

They jumped on the dune buggy and headed straight to the nearest news network. They ran past security guards and raced to the nearest live camera.

"Camels of Melvinopolis, this is what your governor is doing," said Sammy. She then played the footage and shocked 15 million camels.

All the camels went into the city square with signs demanding: "THE GOVERNOR MUST GO".

The next day the congress of Melvinopolis met and impeached the governor, and the police arrested BIG camel.

The kids and Charlie rolled into the center square. The demonstrators asked Charlie to become the new governor: "You were brave and stood up to the bad guys!"

Charlie then told everyone that he did not want to serve. He was going on space journeys with the kids. The demonstrators were sad.

Then their leader said, "We would like to honor you. We declare that, from now on, you should be called Melvin the Camel. We want to tell the universe of your bravery."

"I accept this honor. I am proud to represent Melvinopolis on all of my space missions."

Then the kids and Melvin went to their spaceship and flew away.

The Hot Tub

The spaceship Adventure was blasting across the Milky Way with Lucas as the pilot.

"Oh my Camel!" shouted Lucas. "The planet ahead of us is in deep trouble!"

Melvin ran to the controls "Look

at those ice caps, they're melting at an incredible speed!"

"I'll stay on the spaceship," said Bella. "You guys go on the Explorer and find out what's going on."

Melvin and the other kids ran to the Explorer and hurtled towards the planet. As they approached, they saw thousands of green big-eyed creatures floating in water.

"That's not an ocean," said Cody.

"What is it?" asked Sammy.

"A huge hot tub!" said Lucas.

"What in the world is a hot tub?"

asked Melvin as they landed.

The group left the Explorer and went on the dune buggy. Moving forward on the road, they met a big green creature with an even bigger beach towel. The creature smiled and said, "Gurgle goop giggle grump."

Melvin translated into English: "The great supplier of huge hot tubs, Donald Trump, wants to know the reason for your visit."

"Tell him that we would like to see Donald Trump," said Lucas.

"Gaugle gip giggle grupy," said Melvin.

"Guguly gig," said the creature. Melvin then quickly translated that into English: "He said to follow him."

The kids followed the alien into a huge purple spaceship. The alien then led them into a control room and it soon became very clear that they were leaving.

"Wheels up," said one of the crewmen.

"Thrusters on," said another.

Sammy then noticed Donald Trump sitting in a pilot's chair giving orders left and right.

She raced over to Trump. "Your

hot tub is going to destroy this planet!" yelled Sammy.

"How?!" replied Donald Trump.

"Your hot tub is melting the ice caps of this planet at an enormous rate!"

"Ha, don't tell me that this is another example of that hoax — global warming!"

Donald Trump then pressed a button and Melvin and the kids were thrown out of the ship.

Just as they hit the ground, the Trump ship took off. Bella noticed the ship. She then attempted to radio the group.

"Come in, come in, it's Bella."

Cody got on his radio and said, "Bella, try to capture that ship."

"Why?"

"Because Donald Trump is on that ship and we need him to disconnect the hot tub."

Bella chased the Trump ship and attempted to use a freeze laser to trap it but she missed the first shot. The Trump ship then went into hyper-drive and escaped.

Bella yelled angrily to herself. She

then decided that it would be a good idea to land on the planet and help disable the hot tub in a different way.

When Bella landed, she ran out towards the hot tub.

"Where's Trump?" asked Cody.

"He escaped," said Bella.

The alien then said something in his language, "Gigledy goog gapple gam gig gip gahy gag."

Melvin translated, "Before you explained to Trump the consequences of the hot tub, I did not realize that it was bad. So I have now decided to disable it."

As soon as he said that, everyone ran out of the hot tub screaming and yelling about how cold it was.

Lucas then checked his scanner and realized that the ice caps had stopped melting.

"Th...an...k y...ou," said the alien.

Everyone said their goodbyes and left the planet, ready for their next adventure.

Hellen the Horse

"I'm exhausted," said Melvin. "Let's settle down on a nice planet where I won't stick out."

"How about Earth?" suggested Cody.

"There are lots of different creatures and you'll fit in fine."

"Ok, let's try it," said Melvin.

Sammy flew the Adventure into a patch of trees on Killam's Point, Connecticut. The crunching sound woke up Bruce and Susan Ackerman, the kids' grandparents.

"Is this an invasion?!" asked granddad.

"You'd better check it out," said grandmom.

"How about we both investigate?" said granddad.

They crept up to the Adventure just as Melvin walked out.

"Yikes!" yelled granddad, "What in the world is a camel doing on the East

Coast?" The kids then ran out and grandmom said, "Welcome home from your adventures. How were they?!"

"Very exciting but we now want to settle down for a little while."

"But who's the camel?" asked granddad.

And then Bella explained the entire adventure at Melvinopolis and the encounter with Donald Trump.

"Well, any enemy of Trump is a friend of ours. Melvin, make yourself at home in the garage."

After setting up a camp in the garage, Melvin looked outside and saw a horse running around. He then decided to go and investigate.

"Hi," said Melvin "What's your name?"

The horse was surprised to hear a camel talking horse language. She neighed: "Hi, my name is Hellen. What kind of animal are you? Are you a new kind of horse?"

"I always thought camels and horses were closely related. The only real difference is that I have humps and you don't."

Just at that moment, Hellen's owner, Julius Wimp, called to his horse, "Come over here! Don't you play with camels. They're weird and they're not horses!"

Hellen slowly walked away, turning her head back several times to look again at Melvin. Melvin sadly walked back to the garage, thinking about what he should do.

He met Sammy, who asked, "Why do you look so sad?"

"Because I like a horse named Hellen and her owner took her away, just because I'm a camel, not a horse."

"That's unfair," said Sammy. "Everybody has the right to love whoever they want!"

"But what are we going to do about it?" asked Melvin.

"Meet me at 10 o'clock tonight, and we'll try to see her."

Meanwhile, Hellen was in her stall, crying. When Wimp came to give her hay, she refused to eat. He patted her on the forehead but she angrily turned away. He got angry as well and slammed the barn door as he left.

It got dark and Hellen was still sobbing. At that moment Melvin and Sammy approached the barn door. Sammy opened the door and Melvin happily came in.

"Hi," said Hellen, with a huge smile on her face.

"I thought I would never see you again!!"

"You can't stay in the barn because your owner will kick us out," said Sammy. "Why don't you come with us back to my grandparent's house?"

So Hellen, Melvin and Sammy ran away and told grandmom and granddad what had happened.

"You've got to get out of here before Wimp finds out that you're gone," said grandmom.

"But where should we go?" asked

Hellen and Melvin.

Sammy shouted, "Let's go to the spaceship and leave!"

"Does this mean that I have to leave Earth forever?" asked Hellen.

"No, we can come back whenever you want to," said Melvin. "In that case, LET'S GO!!"

Sammy woke up everyone else and told them what had happened and how they needed to leave. They then told grandmom and granddad goodbye and started walking towards the spaceship. Then, they heard Wimp shout, "Stop where you are! You're stealing my horse!"

They all started running and got to the spaceship with Wimp close behind them.

"5, 4, 3, 2, 1, blast off !"

"STOP YOU ROBBERS!" screamed Wimp.

From the control tower Wimp heard the following message: "Sorry Wimp. This is Hellen. I am leaving of my own free will. Goodbye."

Wimp's face turned red and he shouted, "YOU'LL NEVER GET AWAY WITH THIS!"

But the Adventure was gone.

Donald Trump's Bad Hair Day

Donald Trump was having a bad day. He was scratching and scratching his hair but he couldn't figure out what was wrong.

But what he didn't know was that there were two bugs, Jimmy and Timmy, who were professionals in the art of hair tennis. Hair tennis is basically like tennis, except everything is bug sized and the court is on a person's head. Timmy was about to win, but just when he served the ball, Trump's hand grabbed both of them.

When he opened his hand he saw the two bugs in full tennis gear.

"Who do you think you are, playing tennis on the great Trump's head?"

"We are the greatest tennis players in the universe," said Jimmy.

"In that case," said Trump "I'm going to put you in a tiny rocket and blast you out into the Universe."

So, before Jimmy and Timmy could say 'banana cheeseburgers', they were blasted out of the Trump ship.

After a couple of hours of practicing tennis, Jimmy decided to eat. There was only one problem with this idea: Trump had left no food on the rocket.

"Oh my camel," said Jimmy "We have no food." Timmy ran to the radio and started broadcasting an S.O.S.

Meanwhile on the Adventure, Hellen was confused. "I'm speaking in horse language and you somehow understand me, how come?" asked Hellen.

"Because our spaceship translates some of the languages in the galaxy," said Lucas.

"But I really want to learn English myself," said Hellen.

"Sure," said Melvin, "I'll teach you."

While they were happily chatting, the radio played an urgent S.O.S. call: "S.O.S. S.O.S. we are in urgent need of assistance."

After hearing the message, Cody flew the Adventure towards the micro-rocket.

Meanwhile, the bugs were starving. They could hardly raise their eyes when suddenly a huge claw grabbed them and brought the micro-rocket aboard the Adventure.

"Hi," said Jimmy.

"Thanks for saving us," said Timmy.

"No problem," said Bella. "But we would like to know why you were floating in space."

"Well, we were playing tennis in Donald Trump's hair but he captured us, put us in a micro-rocket and blasted us off of the ship," said Jimmy.

"Oh," said Bella. "Just a question: why were you playing tennis in Donald Trump's hair anyway?"

Timmy then sighed and said, "Because he has the best head for it in the galaxy. And we need to practice on a perfect court for the galactic hair tennis tournament next week."

"Well, we could get you into the Trump ship so you could play on Donald Trump's head again," said Bella.

"Great!" said Jimmy and Timmy very happily.

Cody flew the Adventure to the Trump ship with a cloaking device turned on.

"Ok," he said. "Time to blast your micro-rocket into the Trump ship."

However, Donald Trump had placed a tracking device on the micro-rocket and he knew that they were there.

At that moment the ship shook.

"Oh no, he's shooting freeze rays at us," said Lucas.

"Shields at 50 percent," said Sammy.

Cody then flew towards the Trump ship and shot a mustard cannon at the cockpit, making it impossible for the Trump ship to see without using its radar.

However, the Trump ship did use its radar and it shot the Adventure with 15 freeze ray shots.

"We can't move!" said Cody.

"Oh no, we're going to die!" yelled

Jimmy.

"And I have so much left to live for!" said Hellen.

"No, we're not going to die," said Melvin. "Trump won't kill us."

Trump radioed the Adventure: "Prepare to be boarded."

Bella then picked up the radio and talked to Trump. "Do you have a warrant?"

"Ummm… no, but the Constitution doesn't apply in outer space."

"What about the Intergalactic Constitution! You could get in serious trouble."

"Grrrr, you'll never get away with this." At that moment the Trump ship flew away.

"Woohoo!" said everyone "Hooray for Bella!"

It was at that moment that Melvin realized that Jimmy and Timmy were gone.

"Does anyone know where Jimmy and Timmy are?" asked Melvin.

"While we were frozen, I told Jimmy and Timmy to get in the micro-rocket. I then blasted them at the Trump ship.

They should be in Donald Trump's hair by now," said Lucas.

Meanwhile, Donald Trump picked up the micro-rocket on his radar. He then felt his head start to itch. After he realized what was happening, he screamed: "No, NO, NOOOOOO!"

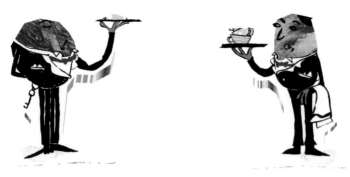

Melotopia

The Adventure stood frozen in outer space. Lucas asked, "How are we going to unfreeze the spaceship?"

"Let's go to the nearest planet and see whether they have some ideas," said Hellen.

So Cody, Bella, Hellen and Melvin went on the Explorer in search of help.

Melvin and Hellen were at the controls and they saw a large orange planet. When they landed, all four of them jumped on the dune buggy and looked around.

They saw a huge living circular thing, with black eyes, big teeth and green skin.

"What in the world is that?!" asked Bella. But before anyone could answer, five of these big things surrounded the dune buggy, lifted it up, and ran with it in the direction of a big city.

Melotopia was enormous. Millions of melons called this place home.

When the kids, Hellen and Melvin arrived, they were stunned by the beautiful colors of all the buildings – red, blue, orange and especially a brilliant green.

But suddenly, they stopped in front of a totally black building. A melon approached and told them to follow him.

The group followed the melon into a gorgeous hotel room.

"This will be your room," said the melon with a British accent.

Before anyone could say anything, the melon walked out, and locked the door.

It was beginning to get late and everyone decided that it was time to go to bed. Everyone's beds were located in different rooms. They all went into their private rooms and went to sleep.

Hellen and Melvin woke up and ordered their breakfast in bed. But when Cody and Bella opened their eyes, they were in an arena with thousands of melons chanting for their death.

"HELP!" yelled Cody.

At that moment, a voice blasted through a microphone.

"You are now in the Melotopia death

arena. Your challenge is simple: survive as many waves of attackers as you can with a freeze gun without being eaten alive by hungry melons."

Meanwhile, Melvin and Hellen were beginning to worry.

"Where have the kids gone?" asked Melvin.

"I can smell them," said Hellen "Follow me".

They started charging toward the death arena.

Cody and Bella thought that they were doomed. Only a miracle could save them. A wave of melons started rolling towards them, their teeth grinding.

At that moment, a miracle happened. Hellen appeared over the arena in a helicopter and threw out a ladder for the kids to hold on to.

But the melons ran up the ladder instead. They opened their mouths and started to eat the helicopter.

"Ahh!" yelled Melvin and Hellen.

Then suddenly, the helicopter blades started chopping the melons into pieces. It was raining melons all over the stadium. The melons on the ground panicked.

Cody and Bella whipped out their ray guns and started freezing them. As the kids jumped on top of the frozen melons, they shouted, "You melons must change your ways, become a functioning part of the universe!"

At that moment, all of the melons realized that the kids were right.

"We shall overcome! How can we

help out our fellow creatures?"

"Well, we could use your help with our spaceship. It's completely frozen and somehow we need to unfreeze it."

"That's funny," said a melon "Freezing technology is our specialty. Consider it done."

After a year of research at Melotopia University, professor Melón and his team flew a space heater into the sky and de-froze the spaceship Adventure. Melotopia had become a functioning and peaceful society.

"Thanks a lot," said Lucas. "We really appreciate it."

The kids and the animals were thanked for their help, and they soon left for their next adventure.

The Fall of Trump

"We got unfrozen just in time," said Lucas.

"What's so special about now?" said Bella.

"It's June 3rd, the day of the galactic hair tennis tournament," said Cody.

"Last year Jimmy and Timmy lost in

the finals to fabulous termites," said Lucas. "But the termites lost in the semi-finals to Wilma and Billma, the greatest cockroach hair tennis duo in history. Since Jimmy and Timmy have squeaked through their match with the grasshoppers, we're set up for the first man vs. woman hair tennis faceoff in history. Pretty cool, right?"

"This year I'm pretty sure that our pals have a huge chance," said Sammy.

"Stop talking and start moving," said Cody, as he moved to the pilot seat. "5,4,3,2,1, blast off!"

After moving into hyper-drive, the

planet Hairosis Tenosis soon became visible on the scanner.

Cody landed the Adventure on Hairosis and everyone stepped out, with two kids on each animal.

"Welcome," said a native Hairling, bowing before them.

The Hairlings were large bugs of an unknown species with huge amounts of hair covering their entire bodies. Except for the big bug eyes in the center of their face, nothing else was visible besides hair.

"Which way to the stadium?" asked Hellen.

A bug jumped on each animal and led the way.

The stadium was an enormous building and it was full of many different creatures.

Everyone took their seats and focused on two tiny bugs who came onto the main tennis hair mat. Then, the two cockroaches entered. Wilma and Billma looked fierce and confident as they towered over the tiny bugs.

"Yikes!" yelled Bella, "I'm not so sure that our pals can beat these monstrous creatures!"

Jimmy threw up the ball and as he

was about to make the first serve when a giant spaceship flew over the stadium. It blasted out, "All you bugs pay attention to me, the great and all-powerful Donald J. Trump!"

"Shut up Trump!" shouted Jimmy, "Can't you see that we're doing something important?"

"You will come with me and never be seen again," said Trump.

"That's what you said the last time," said Timmy. "But this time you can't capture us."

During this conversation, Hellen and Melvin had quietly left the stadium and had blasted off with the Adventure. They aimed the freeze gun at the Trump ship and shot 3 shots, stopping it in its tracks.

"What's going on here!? Who is challenging the almighty Trump?" screamed Donald.

"We knew that you would be coming to capture us, so we decided to make a plan to stop you. You are now under the control of Hellen Horsie and Melvin Camelio," said Timmy.

"That's what you think, but I have a secret de-freezing agent and I will be unfrozen in 15 seconds. I will destroy this entire stadium unless these two rebel bugs are seized and given to me at once!"

In response to this demand, thousands of big bugs rushed onto the tennis court trying to grab Jimmy and Timmy.

As this was happening, Melvin and Hellen boarded the Trump ship and were charging at the crew. After the crew had been dealt with, Hellen and Melvin arrested Trump. Melvin then spoke through the radio and projected his voice across the stadium.

"Donald Trump has been arrested

for his many space crimes against innocent creatures of all types. Now is the time to put him on trial. You yourselves have witnessed him threatening the lives of all the creatures in this stadium. Is this enough to establish his guilt?"

"YES!" shouted all the bugs.

After Donald J. Trump had been arrested and found guilty, he was sentenced to 15 years without money.

"Nooo!" said Trump "Send me to prison, I have to have money to keep buying cool wigs."

But nobody wanted to hear it. He

was given a social security pension, which allowed him only to buy food, a small apartment and other basic necessities.

"Life is terrible!" cried Trump as he microwaved his bean burrito. "I don't have a butler anymore, I could burn my hands. Ouch!"

Finally Trump did something that he said he would do.

They took Donald Trump to the hospital and the TV cameras showed him patiently waiting his turn while other people were being cared for.

A Wedding Invitation

Once Trump had been expelled from the stadium, the two teams got serious.

Whack, whack, whack. The ball sped back and forth between the cockroaches and the bugs. The fans roared. This was the greatest match that they had ever seen.

Five hours passed. The bugs were exhausted and could barely move.

It was tied. The final serve would decide it all. Jimmy was about to throw the ball up when he remembered that he had a cup of coffee in his pocket. He took it out, drank it, had a gigantic energy boost and served an ace past the exhausted cockroaches.

"We won!" yelled Jimmy. "Woohoo!" yelled Timmy.

Wilma and Billma slowly crawled to the net, smiled and shook the hands of Jimmy and Timmy.

Suddenly the Adventure landed, right in the middle of the stadium. While the hundreds of thousands of fans roared their approval, Jimmy and Timmy were awarded the gold statue made from

Trump's treasure.

Hellen and Melvin walked out of the spaceship and handed both Jimmy and Timmy an invitation to their wedding.

Each bug jumped on an animal and they marched triumphantly back into the Adventure.

The fans cheered as the ship blasted off towards earth.

The Grand Finale

The Adventure landed on Killam's Point. Its roar woke up granddad and grandmom.

"Is this an earthquake?" asked granddad.

"Don't be silly," said grandmom,

looking out the window. "It's a spaceship, and the kids are running out with a camel and a horse close behind."

Grandmom and granddad opened the front door and greeted the kids. Everyone marched in, including the animals, saying hi to grandmom and granddad as they passed. Granddad then noticed the bugs on top of Hellen and screamed, "Aieeee!"

"Don't be afraid," said Hellen. "These bugs are some of our closest friends and they are the champions of the universe in hair tennis. We definitely want them to be honored guests at our wedding."

"What wedding?" asked grandmom.

"Oh, we didn't tell you, but we're getting married!" said Melvin.

"Fabulous, can I be the guy who marries you?" asked granddad.

"Definitely, but let's invite everybody on Killam's Point."

When Julius Wimp heard the news, he was outraged. He waited until everybody else – both humans and animals – had gathered on the Secret Beach for the wedding. Hellen arrived on a boat and just as she was greeted by Melvin, Wimp jumped out from behind a bush and said, "I protest, this horse is my private property!"

All of the guests booed, and then Wimp started scratching his hair. His hair itched and itched and he watched the crowd's smiles get bigger.

"You'll never get away with this!" cried Wimp, just before he plunged into the water.

When he came out, his hair was still itching. Granddad explained, "Mr. Wimp, we are living in a new world of equal rights for humans and animals. Just as we got rid of slavery, we are now recognizing animal rights. And the most basic right is to allow two loving animals to love each other as they wish."

Julius Wimp realized that granddad was right and, without saying another word, sat down in the audience and started listening.

As Hellen marched down the aisle to the song "Here Comes The Bride," a large man quietly entered and sat in the back row. It was Donald Trump. His hair was completely gone. But on top of his head, sat Jimmy and Timmy. Donald smiled and let the two bugs jump on his hand and play a little tennis.

"I now pronounce you man and wife," said granddad.

Melvin kissed Hellen and they all lived happily ever after, or so we hope.

Vocabulary:

Corruption: Dishonest behavior by those in power, usually involving bribery.

Impeached: To be fired from being President.

Hoax: Something that isn't real.

Global Warming: An increase in the world's temperature.

Warrant: Official permission to arrest somebody.

Constitution: The basic rules of government.

Equal rights: Everyone has the same rights to the same things.

Slavery: Somebody who is completely bossed around and not paid for doing their work.

65

About the authors:

Cody Sebastian Visnick was born April 16, 2004. Cody was born in Portland, Oregon, to his parents Sybil Ackerman and Marc Visnick. His family soon moved to Connecticut for a year to live with his grandparents Bruce and Susan Ackerman. Ever since he was born he loved to have fun. Nowadays his favorite things to do are to play outside, play sports, play videogames, and read and play with his friends. ***Donald Trump Meets Melvin the Camel*** is his first book but he hopes to write many more in the future.

~

Bruce Ackerman was born on August 19,1943 in the Bronx. He's been a very lucky guy. He met his wife, Susan, when they were both graduate students at Yale, and they've been happily married for almost fifty years. They love to visit with their two kids, Sybil and John, and their fine families. Bruce and Cody have had lots of great times together, and it was a lot of fun writing this book.

50763618R00040

Made in the USA
Middletown, DE
04 November 2017